Temple Trouble

by

H. Beam Piper

Through a haze of incense and altar smoke, Yat-Zar looked down from his golden throne at the end of the dusky, many-pillared temple. Yat-Zar was an idol, of gigantic size and extraordinarily good workmanship; he had three eyes, made of turquoises as big as doorknobs, and six arms. In his three right hands, from top to bottom, he held a sword with a flame-shaped blade, a jeweled object of vaguely phallic appearance, and, by the ears, a rabbit. In his left hands were a bronze torch with burnished copper flames, a big goblet, and a pair of scales with an egg in one pan balanced against a skull in the other. He had a long bifurcate beard made of gold wire, feet like a bird's, and other rather startling anatomical features. His throne was set upon a stone plinth about twenty feet high, into the front of which a doorway opened; behind him was a wooden screen, elaborately gilded and painted.

Directly in front of the idol, Ghullam the high priest knelt on a big blue and gold cushion. He wore a gold-fringed robe of dark blue, and a tall conical gold miter, and a bright blue false beard, forked like the idol's golden one: he was intoning a prayer, and holding up, in both hands, for divine inspection and approval, a long curved knife. Behind him, about thirty feel away, stood a square stone altar, around which four of the lesser priests, in light blue robes with less gold fringe and dark-blue false beards, were busy with the preliminaries to the sacrifice. At considerable distance, about halfway down the length of the temple, some two hundred worshipers—a few substantial citizens in gold-fringed tunics, artisans in tunics without gold fringe, soldiers in mail hauberks and plain steel caps, one officer in ornately gilded armor, a number of peasants in nondescript smocks, and women of all classes—were beginning to prostrate themselves on the stone floor.

Ghullam rose to his feet, bowing deeply to Yat-Zar and holding the knife extended in front of him, and backed away toward the altar. As he did, one of the lesser priests reached into a fringed and embroidered sack and pulled out a live rabbit, a big one, obviously of domestic breed, holding it by the ears while one of his fellows took it by the hind legs. A third priest caught up a silver pitcher, while the fourth fanned the altar fire with a sheet-silver fan. As they began chanting antiphonally, Ghullam turned and quickly whipped the edge of his knife across the rabbit's throat. The priest with the pitcher stepped in to catch the blood, and when the rabbit was bled, it was laid on the fire. Ghullam and his four assistants all shouted together, and the congregation shouted in response.

The high priest waited as long as was decently necessary and then, holding the knife in front of him, stepped around the prayer-cushion and went through the door under the idol into the Holy of Holies. A boy in novice's white robes met him and took the knife, carrying it reverently to a fountain for washing. Eight or ten under-priests, sitting at a long table, rose and bowed, then sat down again and resumed their eating and drinking. At another table, a half-dozen upper priests nodded to him in casual greeting.

Crossing the room, Ghullam went to the Triple Veil in front of the House of Yat-Zar, where only the highest of the priesthood might go, and parted the curtains, passing through, until he came to the great gilded door. Here he fumbled under his robe and produced a small object like a mechanical pencil, inserting the pointed end in a tiny hole in the door and pressing on the other end. The door opened, then swung shut behind him, and as it locked itself, the lights came on within. Ghullam removed his miter and his false beard, tossing them aside on a table, then undid his sash and peeled out of his robe. His regalia discarded, he stood for a moment in loose trousers and a soft white shirt, with a pistollike weapon in a shoulder holster under his left arm—no longer Ghullam the high priest of Yat-Zar, but now Stranor Sleth, resident agent on this time-line of the Fourth Level Proto-Aryan Sector for the Transtemporal Mining Corporation. Then he opened a door at the other side of the anteroom and went to the antigrav shaft, stepping over the edge and floating downward.

There were temples of Yat-Zar on every time-line of the Proto-Aryan Sector, for the worship of Yat-Zar was ancient among the Hulgun people of that area of paratime, but there were only a few which had such installations as this, and all of them were owned and operated by Transtemporal Mining, which had the fissionable ores franchise for this sector. During the ten elapsed centuries since Transtemporal had begun operations on this sector, the process had become standardized. A few First Level paratimers would transpose to a selected time-line and abduct an upper-priest of Yat-Zar, preferably the high priest of the temple at Yoldav or Zurb. He would be drugged and transposed to the First Level, where he would receive hypnotic indoctrination and, while unconscious, have an operation performed on his ears which would enable him to hear sounds well above the normal audible range. He would be able to hear the shrill sonar-cries of bats, for instance, and, more important, he would be able to hear voices when the speaker used a First Level audio-frequency step-up phone. He would also receive a memory-obliteration from the moment of his abduction, and a set of pseudo-memories of a visit to the Heaven of Yat-Zar, on the other side of the sky. Then he would be returned to his own time-line and left on a mountain top far from his temple, where an unknown peasant, leading a donkey, would always find him, return him to the temple, and then vanish inexplicably.

Then the priest would begin hearing voices, usually while serving at the altar. They would warn of future events, which would always come to pass exactly as foretold. Or they might bring tidings of things happening at a distance, the news of which would not arrive by normal means for days or even weeks. Before long, the holy man who had been carried alive to the Heaven of Yat-Zar would acquire a most awesome reputation as a prophet, and would speedily rise to the very top of the priestly hierarchy.

Then he would receive two commandments from Yat-Zar. The first would ordain that all lower priests must travel about from temple to temple, never staying longer than a year at any one place. This would insure a steady influx of newcomers personally unknown to the local upper-priests, and many of them would be First Level paratimers. Then, there would be a second commandment: A house must be built for Yat-Zar, against the rear wall of each temple. Its dimensions were minutely stipulated; its walls were to be of stone, without windows, and there was to be a single door, opening into the Holy of Holies, and before the walls were finished, the door was to be barred from within. A triple veil of brocaded fabric was to be hung in front of this door. Sometimes such innovations met with opposition from the more conservative members of the hierarchy: when they did, the principal objector would be seized with a sudden and violent illness; he would recover if and when he withdrew his objections.

Very shortly after the House of Yat-Zar would be completed, strange noises would be heard from behind the thick walls. Then, after a while, one of the younger priests would announce that he had been commanded in a vision to go behind the veil and knock upon the door. Going behind the curtains, he would use his door-activator to let himself in, and return by paratime-conveyer to the First Level to enjoy a well-earned vacation. When the high priest would follow him behind the veil, after a few hours, and find that he had vanished, it would be announced as a miracle. A week later, an even greater miracle would be announced. The young priest would return from behind the Triple Veil, clad in such raiment as no man had ever seen, and bearing in his hands a strange box. He would announce that Yat-Zar had commanded him to build a new temple in the mountains, at a place to be made known by the voice of the god speaking out of the box.

This time, there would be no doubts and no objections. A procession would set out, headed by the new revelator bearing the box, and when the clicking voice of the god spoke rapidly out of it, the site would be marked and work would begin. No local labor would ever be employed on such temples; the masons and woodworkers would be strangers, come from afar and speaking a strange tongue, and when the temple was completed, they would never be seen to leave it. Men would say that they had been put to death by the priest and buried under the altar to preserve the secrets of the god. And there would always be an idol to preserve the secrets of the god. And there would always be an idol of Yat-Zar, obviously of heavenly origin, since its workmanship was beyond the powers of any local craftsman. The priests of such a temple would be exempt, by divine decree, from the rule of yearly travel.

Nobody, of course, would have the least idea that there was a uranium mine in operation under it, shipping ore to another time-line. The Hulgun people knew nothing about uranium, and neither did they as much as dream that there were other time-lines. The secret of paratime transposition belonged exclusively to the First Level civilization which had discovered it, and it was a secret that was guarded well.

Stranor Sleth, dropping to the bottom of the antigrav shaft, cast a hasty and instinctive glance to the right, where the freight conveyers were. One was gone, taking its cargo over hundreds of thousands of para-years to the First Level. Another had just returned, empty, and a third was receiving its cargo from the robot mining machines far back under the mountain. Two young men and a girl, in First Level costumes, sat at a bank of instruments and visor-screens, handling the whole operation, and six or seven armed guards, having inspected the newly-arrived conveyer and finding that it had picked up nothing inimical en route, were relaxing and lighting cigarettes. Three of them, Stranor Sleth noticed, wore the green uniforms of the Paratime Police.

"When did those fellows get in?" he asked the people at the control desk, nodding toward the green-clad newcomers.

"About ten minutes ago, on the passenger conveyer," the girl told him. "The Big Boy's here. Brannad Klav. And a Paratime Police officer. They're in your office."

"Uh huh; I was expecting that," Stranor Sleth nodded. Then he turned down the corridor to the left.

Two men were waiting for him, in his office. One was short and stocky, with an angry, impatient face—Brannad Klav, Transtemporal's vice president in charge of operations. The other was tall and slender with handsome and entirely expressionless features; he wore a Paratime Police officer's uniform, with the blue badge of hereditary nobility on his breast, and carried a sigma-ray needler in a belt holster.

"Were you waiting long, gentlemen?" Stranor Sleth asked. "I was holding Sunset Sacrifice up in the temple."

"No, we just got here," Brannad Klav said. "This is Verkan Vall, Mavrad of Nerros, special assistant to Chief Tortha of the Paratime Police, Stranor Sleth, our resident agent here."

Stranor Sleth touched hands with Verkan Vall.

"I've heard a lot about you, sir," he said. "Everybody working in paratime has, of course. I'm sorry we have a situation here that calls for your presence, but since we have, I'm glad you're here in person. You know what our trouble is, I suppose?"

"In a general way," Verkan Vall replied. "Chief Tortha, and Brannad Klav, have given me the main outline, but I'd like to have you fill in the details."

Illustration

"Well, I told you everything," Brannad Klav interrupted impatiently. "It's just that Stranor's let this blasted local king, Kurchuk, get out of control. If I—" He stopped short, catching sight of the shoulder holster under Stranor Sleth's left arm. "Were you wearing that needler up in the temple?" he demanded.

"You're blasted right I was!" Stranor Sleth retorted. "And any time I can't arm myself for my own protection on this time-line, you can have my resignation. I'm not getting into the same jam as those people at Zurb."

"Well, never mind about that," Verkan Vall intervened. "Of course Stranor Sleth has a right to arm himself; I wouldn't think of being caught without a weapon on this time-line, myself.

Now, Stranor, suppose you tell me what's been happening, here, from the beginning of this trouble."

"It started, really, about five years ago, when Kurchuk, the King of Zurb, married this Chuldun princess, Darith, from the country over beyond the Black Sea, and made her his queen, over the heads of about a dozen daughters of the local nobility, whom he'd married previously. Then he brought in this Chuldun scribe, Labdurg, and made him Overseer of the Kingdom—roughly, prime minister. There was a lot of dissatisfaction about that, and for a while it looked as though he was going to have a revolution on his hands, but he brought in about five thousand Chuldun mercenaries, all archers—these Hulguns can't shoot a bow worth beans—so the dissatisfaction died down, and so did most of the leaders of the disaffected group. The story I get is that this Labdurg arranged the marriage, in the first place. It looks to me as though the Chuldun emperor is intending to take over the Hulgun kingdoms, starting with Zurb.

"Well, these Chulduns all worship a god called Muz-Azin. Muz-Azin is a crocodile with wings like a bat and a lot of knife blades in his tail. He makes this Yat-Zar look downright beautiful. So do his habits. Muz-Azin fancies human sacrifices. The victims are strung up by the ankles on a triangular frame and lashed to death with iron-barbed whips. Nasty sort of a deity, but this is a nasty time-line. The people here get a big kick out of watching these sacrifices. Much better show than our bunny-killing. The victims are usually criminals, or overage or incorrigible slaves, or prisoners of war.

"Of course, when the Chulduns began infiltrating the palace, they brought in their crocodile-god, too, and a flock of priests, and King Kurchuk let them set up a temple in the palace. Naturally, we preached against this heathen idolatry in our temples, but religious bigotry isn't one of the numerous imperfections of this sector. Everybody's deity is as good as anybody else's—indifferentism, I believe, is the theological term. Anyhow, on that basis things went along fairly well, till two years ago, when we had this run of bad luck."

"Bad luck!" Brannad Klav snorted. "That's the standing excuse of every incompetent!"

"Go on, Stranor; what sort of bad luck?" Verkan Vall asked.

"Well, first we had a drought, beginning in early summer, that burned up most of the grain crop. Then, when that broke, we got heavy rains and hailstorms and floods, and that destroyed what got through the dry spell. When they harvested what little was left, it was obvious there'd be a famine, so we brought in a lot of grain by conveyer and distributed it from the temples— miraculous gift of Yat-Zar, of course. Then the main office on First Level got scared about flooding this time-line with a lot of unaccountable grain and were afraid we'd make the people suspicious, and ordered it stopped.

"Then Kurchuk, and I might add that the kingdom of Zurb was the hardest hit by the famine, ordered his army mobilized and started an invasion of the Jumdun country, south of the Carpathians, to get grain. He got his army chopped up, and only about a quarter of them got back, with no grain. You ask me, I'd say that Labdurg framed it to happen that way. He advised Kurchuk to invade, in the first place, and I mentioned my suspicion that Chombrog, the Chuldun Emperor, is planning to move in on the Hulgun kingdoms. Well, what would be smarter than to get Kurchuk's army smashed in advance?"

"How did the defeat occur?" Verkan Vall asked. "Any suspicion of treachery?"

"Nothing you could put your finger on, except that the Jumduns seemed to have pretty good intelligence about Kurchuk's invasion route and battle plans. It could have been nothing worse than stupid tactics on Kurchuk's part. See, these Hulguns, and particularly the Zurb Hulguns, are spearmen. They fight in a fairly thin line, with heavy-armed infantry in front and light infantry with throwing-spears behind. The nobles fight in light chariots, usually at the center of the line, and that's where they were at this Battle of Jorm. Kurchuk himself was at the center, with his Chuldun archers massed around him.

"The Jumduns use a lot of cavalry, with long swords and lances, and a lot of big chariots with two javelin men and a driver. Well, instead of ramming into Kurchuk's center, where he had his archers, they hit the extreme left and folded it up, and then swung around behind and hit the right from the rear. All the Chuldun archers did was stand fast around the king and shoot anybody who came close to them: they were left pretty much alone. But the Hulgun spearmen were cut to pieces. The battle ended with Kurchuk and his nobles and his archers making a fighting retreat, while the Jumdun cavalry were chasing the spearmen every which way and cutting them down or lancing them as they ran.

"Well, whether it was Labdurg's treachery or Kurchuk's stupidity, in either case, it was natural for the archers to come off easiest and the Hulgun spearmen to pay the butcher's bill. But try and tell these knuckle-heads anything like that! Muz-Azin protected the Chulduns, and Yat-Zar let the Hulguns down, and that was all there was to it. The Zurb temple started losing worshipers, particularly the families of the men who didn't make it back from Jorm.

"If that had been all there'd been to it, though, it still wouldn't have hurt the mining operations, and we could have got by. But what really tore it was when the rabbits started to die." Stranor Sleth picked up a cigar from his desk and bit the end, spitting it out disgustedly. "Tularemia, of course," he said, touching his lighter to the tip. "When that hit, they started going over to Muz-Azin in droves, not only at Zurb but all over the Six Kingdoms. You ought to have seen the house we had for Sunset Sacrifice, this evening! About two hundred, and we used to get two thousand. It used to be all two men could do to lift the offering box at the door, afterward, and all the money we took in tonight I could put in one pocket!" The high priest used language that would have been considered unclerical even among the Hulguns.

Verkan Vall nodded. Even without the quickie hypno-mech he had taken for this sector, he knew that the rabbit was domesticated among the Proto-Aryan Hulguns and was their chief meat animal. Hulgun rabbits were even a minor import on the First Level, and could be had at all the better restaurants in cities like Dhergabar. He mentioned that.

"That's not the worst of it," Stranor Sleth told him. "See, the rabbit's sacred to Yat-Zar. Not taboo; just sacred. They have to use a specially consecrated knife to kill them—consecrating rabbit knives has always been an item of temple revenue—and they must say a special prayer before eating them. We could have got around the rest of it, even the Battle of Jorm—punishment by Yat-Zar for the sin of apostasy—but Yat-Zar just wouldn't make rabbits sick. Yat-Zar thinks too well of rabbits to do that, and it'd not been any use claiming he would. So there you are."

"Well, I take the attitude that this situation is the result of your incompetence," Brannad Klav began, in a bullyragging tone. "You're not only the high priest of this temple, you're the acknowledged head of the religion in all the Hulgun kingdoms. You should have had more hold on the people than to allow anything like this to happen."

"Hold on the people!" Stranor Sleth fairly howled, appealing to Verkan Vall. "What does he think a religion is, on this sector, anyhow? You think these savages dreamed up that six-armed monstrosity, up there, to express their yearning for higher things, or to symbolize their moral ethos, or as a philosophical escape-hatch from the dilemma of causation? They never even heard of such matters. On this sector, gods are strictly utilitarian. As long as they take care of their worshipers, they get their sacrifices: when they can't put out, they have to get out. How do you suppose these Chulduns, living in the Caucasus Mountains, got the idea of a god like a crocodile, anyhow? Why, they got it from Homran traders, people from down in the Nile Valley. They had a god, once, something basically like a billy goat, but he let them get licked in a couple of battles, so out he went. Why, all the deities on this sector have hyphenated names, because they're combinations of several deities, worshiped in one person. Do you know anything about the history of this sector?" he asked the Paratime Police officer.

"Well, it develops from an alternate probability of what we call the Nilo-Mesopotamian Basic sector-group," Verkan Vall said. "On most Nilo-Mesopotamian sectors, like the Macedonian Empire Sector, or the Alexandrian-Roman or Alexandrian-Punic or Indo-Turanian or Europo-American, there was an Aryan invasion of Eastern Europe and Asia Minor about four thousand elapsed years ago. On this sector, the ancestors of the Aryans came in about fifteen centuries earlier, as neolithic savages, about the time that the Sumerian and Egyptian civilizations were first developing, and overran all southeast Europe, Asia Minor and the Nile Valley. They developed to the bronze-age culture of the civilizations they overthrew, and then, more slowly, to an iron-age culture. About two thousand years ago, they were using hardened steel and building large stone cities, just as they do now. At that time, they reached cultural stasis. But as for their religious beliefs, you've described them quite accurately. A god is only worshiped as long as the people think him powerful enough to aid and protect them; when they lose that confidence, he is discarded and the god of some neighboring people is adopted instead." He turned to Brannad Klav. "Didn't Stranor report this situation to you when it first developed?" he asked. "I know he did; he speaks of receiving shipments of grain by conveyer for temple distribution. Then why didn't you report it to Paratime Police? That's what we have a Paratime Police Force for."

"Well, yes, of course, but I had enough confidence in Stranor Sleth to think that he could handle the situation himself. I didn't know he'd gone slack—"

"Look, I can't make weather, even if my parishioners think I can," Stranor Sleth defended himself. "And I can't make a great military genius out of a blockhead like Kurchuk. And I can't immunize all the rabbits on this time-line against tularemia, even if I'd had any reason to expect a tularemia epidemic, which I hadn't because the disease is unknown on this sector; this is the only outbreak of it anybody's ever heard of on any Proto-Aryan time-line."

"No, but I'll tell you what you could have done," Verkan Vall told him. "When this Kurchuk started to apostatize, you could have gone to him at the head of a procession of priests, all paratimers and all armed with energy-weapons, and pointed out his spiritual duty to him, and if he gave you any back talk, you could have pulled out that needler and rayed him down and then cried, 'Behold the vengeance of Yat-Zar upon the wicked king!' I'll bet any sum at any odds that his successor would have thought twice about going over to Muz-Azin, and none of these other kings would have even thought once about it."

"Ha, that's what I wanted to do!" Stranor Sleth exclaimed. "And who stopped me? I'll give you just one guess."

"Well, it seems there was slackness here, but it wasn't Stranor Sleth who was slack," Verkan Vall commented.

"Well! I must say; I never thought I'd hear an officer of the Paratime Police criticizing me for trying to operate inside the Paratime Transposition Code!" Brannad Klav exclaimed.

Verkan Vall, sitting on the edge of Stranor Sleth's desk, aimed his cigarette at Brannad Klav like a blaster.

Illustration

"Now, look," he began. "There is one, and only one, inflexible law regarding outtime activities. The secret of paratime transposition must be kept inviolate, and any activity tending to endanger it is prohibited. That's why we don't allow the transposition of any object of extraterrestrial origin to any time-line on which space travel has not been developed. Such an object may be preserved, and then, after the local population begin exploring the planet from whence it came, there will be dangerous speculations and theories as to how it arrived on Terra at such an early date. I came within inches, literally, of getting myself killed, not long ago, cleaning up the result of a violation of that regulation. For the same reason, we don't allow the export, to outtime natives, of manufactured goods too far in advance of their local culture. That's why, for instance, you people have to hand-finish all those big Yat-Zar idols, to remove traces of machine work. One of those things may be around, a few thousand years from now, when these people develop a mechanical civilization. But as far as raying down this Kurchuk is concerned, these Hulguns are completely nonscientific. They wouldn't have the least idea what happened. They'd believe that Yat-Zar struck him dead, as gods on this plane of culture are supposed to do, and if any of them noticed the needler at all, they'd think it was just a holy amulet of some kind."

"But the law is the law—" Brannad Klav began.

Verkan Vall shook his head. "Brannad, as I understand, you were promoted to your present position on the retirement of Salvan Marth, about ten years ago; up to that time, you were in your company's financial department. You were accustomed to working subject to the First Level Commercial Regulation Code. Now, any law binding upon our people at home, on the First Level, is inflexible. It has to be. We found out, over fifty centuries ago, that laws have to be rigid and without discretionary powers in administration in order that people may be able to predict their effect and plan their activities accordingly. Naturally, you became conditioned to operating in such a climate of legal inflexibility.

"But in paratime, the situation is entirely different. There exist, within the range of the Ghaldron-Hesthor paratemporal-field generator, a number of time-lines of the order of ten to the hundred-thousandth power. In effect, that many different worlds. In the past ten thousand years, we have visited only the tiniest fraction of these, but we have found everything from time-lines inhabited only by subhuman ape-men to Second Level civilizations which are our own equal in every respect but knowledge of paratemporal transposition. We even know of one Second Level civilization which is approaching the discovery of an interstellar hyperspatial drive, something we've never even come close to. And in between are every degree of savagery, barbarism and civilization. Now, it's just not possible to frame any single code of laws applicable to conditions on all of these.

The best we can do is prohibit certain flagrantly immoral types of activity, such as slave-trading, introduction of new types of narcotic drugs, or out-and-out piracy and brigandage. If you're in doubt as to the legality of anything you want to do outtime, go to the Judicial Section of the Paratime Commission and get an opinion on it. That's where you made your whole mistake. You didn't find out just how far it was allowable for you to go."

He turned to Stranor Sleth again. "Well, that's the background, then. Now tell me about what happened yesterday at Zurb."

"Well, a week ago, Kurchuk came out with this decree closing our temple at Zurb and ordering his subjects to perform worship and make money offerings to Muz-Azin. The Zurb temple isn't a mask for a mine: Zurb's too far south for the uranium deposits. It's just a center for propaganda and that sort of thing. But they have a House of Yat-Zar, and a conveyer, and most of the upper-priests are paratimers. Well, our man there, Tammand Drav, alias Khoram, defied the king's order, so Kurchuk sent a company of Chuldun archers to close the temple and arrest the priests. Tammand Drav got all his people who were in the temple at the time into the House of Yat-Zar and transposed them back to the First Level. He had orders"—Stranor Sleth looked meaningly at Brannad Klav—"not to resist with energy-weapons or even ultrasonic paralyzers. And while we're on the subject of letting the local yokels see too much, about fifteen of the under-priests he took to the First Level were Hulgun natives."

"Nothing wrong about that: they'll get memory-obliteration and pseudo-memory treatment," Verkan Vall said. "But he should have been allowed to needle about a dozen of those Chulduns. Teach the beggars to respect Yat-Zar in the future. Now, how about the six priests who were outside the temple at the time? All but one were paratimers. We'll have to find out about them, and get them out of Zurb."

"That'll take some doing," Stranor Sleth said. "And it'll have to be done before sunset tomorrow. They are all in the dungeon of the palace citadel, and Kurchuk is going to give them to the priests of Muz-Azin to be sacrificed tomorrow evening."

"How'd you learn that?" Verkan Vall asked.

"Oh, we have a man in Zurb, not connected with the temple," Stranor Sleth said. "Name's Crannar Jurth; calls himself Kranjur, locally. He has a swordmaker's shop, employs about a dozen native journeymen and apprentices who hammer out the common blades he sells in the open market. Then, he imports a few high-class alloy-steel blades from the First Level, that'll cut through this local low-carbon armor like cheese. Fits them with locally-made hilts and sells them at unbelievable prices to the nobility. He's Swordsmith to the King; picks up all the inside palace dope. Of course, he was among the first to accept the New Gospel and go over to Muz-Azin. He has a secret room under his shop, with his conveyer and a radio.

"What happened was this: These six priests were at a consecration ceremony at a rabbit-ranch outside the city, and they didn't know about the raid on the temple. On their way back, they were surrounded by Chuldun archers and taken prisoner. They had no weapons but their sacrificial knives." He threw another dirty look at Brannad Klav. "So they're due to go up on the triangles at sunset tomorrow."

"We'll have to get them out before then," Verkan Vall stated. "They're our people, and we can't let them down; even the native is under our protection, whether he knows it or not. And in the second place, if those priests are sacrificed to Muz-Azin," he told Brannad Klav, "you can shut down everything on this time-line, pull out or disintegrate your installations, and fill in your mine-tunnels. Yat-Zar will be through on this time-line, and you'll be through along with him. And considering that your fissionables franchise for this sector comes up for renewal next year, your company will be through in this paratime area."

"You believe that would happen?" Brannad Klav asked anxiously.

"I know it will, because I'll put through a recommendation to that effect, if those six men are tortured to death tomorrow,"

Verkan Vall replied. "And in the fifty years that I've been in the Police Department, I've only heard of five such recommendations being ignored by the commission. You know, Fourth Level Mineral Products Syndicate is after your franchise. Ordinarily, they wouldn't have a chance of getting it, but with this, maybe they will, even without my recommendation. This was all your fault, for ignoring Stranor Sleth's proposal and for denying those men the right to carry energy weapons."

"Well, we were only trying to stay inside the Paratime Code," Brannad Klav pleaded. "If it isn't too late, now, you can count on me for every co-operation." He fiddled with some papers on the desk. "What do you want me to do to help?"

"I'll tell you that in a minute." Verkan Vall walked to the wall and looked at the map, then returned to Stranor Sleth's desk. "How about these dungeons?" he asked. "How are they located, and how can we get in to them?"

"I'm afraid we can't," Stranor Sleth told him. "Not without fighting our way in. They're under the palace citadel, a hundred feet below ground. They're spatially co-existent with the heavy water barriers around one of our company's plutonium piles on the First Level, and below surface on any unoccupied time-line I know of, so we can't transpose in to them. This palace is really a walled city inside a city. Here, I'll show you."

Going around the desk, he sat down and, after looking in the index-screen, punched a combination on the keyboard. A picture, projected from the microfilm-bank, appeared on the view-screen. It was an air-view of the city of Zurb—taken, the high priest explained, by infrared light from an airboat over the city at night. It showed a city of an entirely pre-mechanical civilization, with narrow streets, lined on either side by low one and two story buildings. Although there would be considerable snow in winter, the roofs were usually flat, probably massive stone slabs supported by pillars within. Even in the poorer sections, this was true except for the very meanest houses and out-buildings, which were thatched. Here and there, some huge pile of masonry would rear itself above its lower neighbors, and, where the streets were wider, occasional groups of large buildings would be surrounded by battlemented walls. Stranor Sleth indicated one of the larger of these.

"Here's the palace," he said. "And here's the temple of Yat-Zar, about half a mile away." He touched a large building, occupying an entire block; between it and the palace was a block-wide park, with lawns and trees on either side of a wide roadway connecting the two.

"Now, here's a detailed view of the palace." He punched another combination; the view of the City was replaced by one, taken from directly overhead, of the walled palace area. "Here's the main gate, in front, at the end of the road from the temple," he pointed out. "Over here, on the left, are the slaves' quarters and the stables and workshops and store houses and so on. Over here, on the other side, are the nobles' quarters. And this,"—he indicated a towering structure at the rear of the walled enclosure—"is the citadel and the royal dwelling. Audience hall on this side; harem over here on this side. A wide stone platform, about fifteen feet high, runs completely across the front of the citadel, from the audience hall to the harem. Since this picture was taken, the new temple of Muz-Azin was built right about here." He indicated that it extended out from the audience hall into the central courtyard. "And out here on the platform, they've put up about a dozen of these triangles, about twelve feet high, on which the sacrificial victims are whipped to death."

"Yes. About the only way we could get down to the dungeons would be to make an airdrop onto the citadel roof and fight our way down with needlers and blasters, and I'm not willing to do that as long as there's any other way," Verkan Vall said. "We'd lose men, even with needlers against bows, and there's a chance that some of our equipment might be lost in the melee and fall into outtime hands. You say this sacrifice comes off tomorrow at sunset?"

"That would be about actual sunset plus or minus an hour; these people aren't astronomers, they don't even have good sundials, and it might be a cloudy day," Stranor Sleth said.

"There will be a big idol of Muz-Azin on a cart, set about here." He pointed. "After the sacrifice, it is to be dragged down this road, outside, to the temple of Yat-Zar, and set up there. The temple is now occupied by about twenty Chuldun mercenaries and five or six priests of Muz-Azin. They haven't, of course, got into the House of Yat-Zar; the door's of impervium steel, about six inches thick, with a plating of collapsed nickel under the gilding. It would take a couple of hours to cut through it with our best atomic torch; there isn't a tool on this time-line that could even scratch it. And the insides of the walls are lined with the same thing."

"Do you think our people have been tortured, yet?" Verkan Vall asked.

"No." Stranor Sleth was positive. "They'll be fairly well treated, until the sacrifice. The idea's to make them last as long as possible on the triangles; Muz-Azin likes to see a slow killing, and so does the mob of spectators."

"That's good. Now, here's my plan. We won't try to rescue them from the dungeons. Instead, we'll transpose back to the Zurb temple from the First Level, in considerable force—say a hundred or so men—and march on the palace, to force their release. You're in constant radio communication with all the other temples on this time-line, I suppose?"

Illustration

"Yes, certainly."

"All right. Pass this out to everybody, authority Paratime Police, in my name, acting for Tortha Karf. I want all paratimers who can possibly be spared to transpose to First Level immediately and rendezvous at the First Level terminal of the Zurb temple conveyer as soon as possible. Close down all mining operations, and turn over temple routine to the native under-priests. You can tell them that the upper-priests are retiring to their respective Houses of Yat-Zar to pray for the deliverance of the priests in the hands of King Kurchuk. And everybody is to bring back his priestly regalia to the First Level;

that will be needed." He turned to Brannad Klav. "I suppose you keep spare regalia in stock on the First Level?"

"Yes, of course; we keep plenty of everything in stock. Robes, miters, false beards of different shades, everything."

"And these big Yat-Zar idols: they're mass-produced on the First Level? You have one available now? Good. I'll want some alterations made on one. For one thing, I'll want it plated heavily, all over, with collapsed nickel. For another, I'll want it fitted with antigrav units and some sort of propulsion-units, and a loudspeaker, and remote control.

"And, Stranor, you get in touch with this swordmaker, Crannar Jurth, and alert him to co-operate with us. Tell him to start calling Zurb temple on his radio about noon tomorrow, and keep it up till he gets an answer. Or, better, tell him to run his conveyer to his First Level terminal, and bring with him an extra suit of clothes appropriate to the role of journeyman-mechanic. I'll want to talk to him, and furnish him with special equipment. Got all that? Well, carry on with it, and bring your own paratimers, priests and mining operators, back with you as soon as you've taken care of everything. Brannad, you come with me, now. We're returning to First Level immediately. We have a lot of work to do, so let's get started."

"Anything I can do to help, just call on me for it," Brannad Klav promised earnestly. "And, Stranor, I want to apologize. I'll admit, now, that I ought to have followed your recommendations, when this situation first developed."

By noon of the next day, Verkan Vall had at least a hundred men gathered in the big room at the First Level fissionables refinery at Jarnabar, spatially co-existent with the Fourth Level temple of Yat-Zar at Zurb. He was having a little trouble distinguishing between them, for every man wore the fringed blue robe and golden miter of an upper-priest, and had his face masked behind a blue false beard. It was, he admitted to himself, a most ludicrous-looking assemblage; one of the most ludicrous things about it was the fact that it would have inspired only pious awe in a Hulgun of the Fourth Level Proto-Aryan Sector. About half of them were priests from the Transtemporal Mining Corporation's temples; the other half were members of the Paratime Police. All of them wore, in addition to their temple knives, holstered sigma-ray needlers. Most of them carried ultrasonic paralyzers, eighteen-inch batonlike things with bulbous ends. Most of the Paratime Police and a few of the priests also carried either heat-ray pistols or neutron-disruption blasters; Verkan Vall wore one of the latter in a left-hand belt holster.

The Paratime Police were lined up separately for inspection, and Stranor Sleth, Tammand Drav of the Zurb temple, and several other high priests were checking the authenticity of their disguises. A little apart from the others, a Paratime Policeman, in high priest's robes and beard, had a square box slung in front of him; he was fiddling with knobs and buttons on it, practicing. A big idol of Yat-Zar, on antigravity, was floating slowly about the room in obedience to its remote controls, rising and lowering, turning about and pirouetting gracefully.

"Hey, Vall!" he called to his superior. "How's this?"

The idol rose about five feet, turned slowly in a half-circle, moved to the right a little, and then settled slowly toward the floor.

"Fine, fine, Horv," Verkan Vall told him, "but don't set it down on anything, or turn off the antigravity. There's enough collapsed nickel-plating on that thing to sink it a yard in soft ground."

"I don't know what the idea of that was," Brannad Klav, standing beside him, said. "Understand, I'm not criticizing. I haven't any right to, under the circumstances. But it seems to me that armoring that thing in collapsed nickel was an unnecessary precaution."

"Maybe it was," Verkan Vall agreed. "I sincerely hope so. But we can't take any chances. This operation has to be absolutely right. Ready, Tammand? All right; first detail into the conveyer."

He turned and strode toward a big dome of fine metallic mesh, thirty feet high and sixty in diameter, at the other end of the room. Tammand Drav, and his ten paratimer priests, and Brannad Klav, and ten Paratime Police, followed him in. One of the latter slid shut the door and locked it; Verkan Vall went to the control desk, at the center of the dome, and picked up a two-foot globe of the same fine metallic mesh, opening it and making some adjustments inside, then attaching an electric cord and closing it. He laid the globe on the floor near the desk and picked up the hand battery at the other end of the attached cord.

"Not taking any chances at all, are you?" Brannad Klav asked, watching this operation with interest.

"I never do, unnecessarily. There are too many necessary chances that have to be taken, in this work." Verkan Vall pressed the button on the hand battery. The globe on the floor flashed and vanished. "Yesterday, five paratimers were arrested. Any or all of them could have had door-activators with them. Stranor Sleth says they were not tortured, but that is a purely inferential statement. They may have been, and the use of the activator may have been extorted from one of them. So I want a look at the inside of that conveyer-chamber before we transpose into it."

He laid the hand battery, with the loose-dangling wire that had been left behind, on the desk, then lit a cigarette. The others gathered around, smoking and watching, careful to avoid the place from which the globe had vanished. Thirty minutes passed, and then, in a queer iridescence, the globe reappeared. Verkan Vall counted ten seconds and picked it up, taking it to the desk and opening it to remove a small square box. This he slid into a space under the desk and flipped a switch. Instantly, a view-screen lit up and a three-dimensional picture appeared—the interior of a big room a hundred feet square and some seventy in height. There was a big desk and a radio; tables, couches, chairs and an arms-rack full of weapons, and at one end, a remarkably clean sixty-foot circle on the concrete floor, outlined in faintly luminous red.

"How about it?" Verkan Vall asked Tammand Drav. "Anything wrong?"

The Zurb high priest shook his head. "Just as we left it," he said. "Nobody's been inside since we left."

One of the policemen took Verkan Vall's place at the control desk and threw the master switch, after checking the instruments. Immediately, the paratemporal-transposition field went on with a humming sound that mounted to a high scream, then settled to a steady drone. The mesh dome flickered with a cold iridescence and vanished, and they were looking into the interior of a great fissionables refinery plant, operated by paratimers on another First Level time-line. The structural details altered, from time-line to time-line, as they watched. Buildings appeared and vanished. Once, for a few seconds, they were inside a cool, insulated bubble in the midst of molten lead. Tammand Drav jerked a thumb at it, before it vanished.

"That always bothers me," he said. "Bad place for the field to go weak. I'm fussy as an old hen about inspection of the conveyer, on account of that."

"Don't blame you," Verkan Vall agreed. "Probably the cooling system of a breeder-pile."

They passed more swiftly, now, across the Second Level and the Third. Once they were in the midst of a huge land battle, with great tanklike vehicles spouting flame at one another. Another moment was spent in an air bombardment. On any time-line, this section of East Europe was a natural battleground. Once a great procession marched toward them, carrying red banners and huge pictures of a coarse-faced man with a black mustache—Verkan Vall recognized the environment as Fourth Level Europo-American Sector. Finally, as the transposition-rate slowed, they saw a clutter of miserable thatched huts, in the rear of a granite wall of a Fourth Level Hulgun temple of Yat-Zar— a temple not yet infiltrated by Transtemporal Mining Corporation agents. Finally, they were at their destination. The dome around them became visible, and an overhead green light flashed slowly on and off.

Verkan Vall opened the door and stepped outside, his needler drawn. The House of Yat-Zar was just as he had seen it in the picture photographed by the automatic reconnaissance-conveyer. The others crowded outside after him. One of the regular priests pulled off his miter and beard and went to the radio, putting on a headset. Verkan Vall and Tammand Drav snapped on the visiscreen, getting a view of the Holy of Holies outside.

There were six men there, seated at the upper-priests' banquet table, drinking from golden goblets. Five of them wore the black robes with green facings which marked them as priests of Muz-Azin; the sixth was an officer of the Chuldun archers, in gilded mail and helmet.

"Why, those are the sacred vessels of the temple!" Tammand Drav cried, scandalized. Then he laughed in self-ridicule. "I'm beginning to take this stuff seriously, myself; time I put in for a long vacation. I was actually shocked at the sacrilege!"

"Well, let's overtake the infidels in their sins," Verkan Vall said. "Paralyzers will be good enough."

He picked up one of the bulb-headed weapons, and unlocked the door. Tammand Drav and another of the priests of the Zurb temple following and the others crowding behind, they passed out through the veils, and burst into the Holy of Holies. Verkan Vall pointed the bulb of his paralyzer at the six seated men and pressed the button; other paralyzers came into action, and the whole sextet were knocked senseless. The officer rolled from his chair and fell to the floor in a clatter of armor. Two of the priests slumped forward on the table. The others merely sank back in their chairs, dropping their goblets.

"Give each one of them another dose, to make sure," Verkan Vall directed a couple of his own men. "Now, Tammand; any other way into the main temple beside that door?"

"Up those steps," Tammand Drav pointed. "There's a gallery along the side; we can cover the whole room from there."

"Take your men and go up there. I'll take a few through the door. There'll be about twenty archers out there, and we don't want any of them loosing any arrows before we can knock them out. Three minutes be time enough?"

"Easily. Make it two," Tammand Drav said.

He took his priests up the stairway and vanished into the gallery of the temple. Verkan Vall waited until one minute had passed and then, followed by Brannad Klav and a couple of Paratime Policemen, he went under the plinth and peered out into the temple. Five or six archers, in steel caps and sleeveless leather jackets sewn with steel rings, were gathered around the altar, cooking something in a pot on the fire. Most of the others, like veteran soldiers, were sprawled on the floor, trying to catch a short nap, except half a dozen, who crouched in a circle, playing some game with dice—another almost universal military practice.

The two minutes were up. He aimed his paralyzer at the men around the altar and squeezed the button, swinging it from one to another and knocking them down with a bludgeon of inaudible sound. At the same time, Tammand Drav and his detail were stunning the gamblers. Stepping forward and to one side, Verkan Vall, Brannad Klav and the others took care of the sleepers on the floor. In less than thirty seconds, every Chuldun in the temple was incapacitated.

"All right, make sure none of them come out of it prematurely," Verkan Vall directed. "Get their weapons, and be sure nobody has a knife or anything hidden on him. Who has the syringe and the sleep-drug ampoules?"

Somebody had, it developed, who was still on the First Level, to come up with the second conveyer load. Verkan Vall swore. Something like this always happened, on any operation involving more than half a dozen men.

"Well, some of you stay here: patrol around, and use your paralyzers on anybody who even twitches a muscle." Ultrasonics were nice, effective, humane police weapons, but they were unreliable. The same dose that would keep one man out for an hour would paralyze another for no more than ten or fifteen minutes. "And be sure none of them are playing 'possum."

He went back through the door under the plinth, glancing up at the decorated wooden screen and wondering how much work it would take to move the new Yat-Zar in from the conveyers. The five priests and the archer-captain were still unconscious; one of the policemen was searching them.

"Here's the sort of weapons these priests carry," he said, holding up a short iron mace with a spiked head. "Carry them on their belts." He tossed it on the table, and began searching another knocked-out hierophant. "Like this—*Hey!* Look at this, will you!"

He drew his hand from under the left side of the senseless man's robe and held up a sigma-ray needler. Verkan Vall looked at it and nodded grimly.

"Had it in a regular shoulder holster," the policeman said, handing the weapon across the table. "What do you think?"

"Find anything else funny on him?"

"Wait a minute." The policeman pulled open the robe and began stripping the priest of Muz-Azin; Verkan Vall came around the table to help. There was nothing else of a suspicious nature.

"Could have got it from one of the prisoners, but I don't like the familiar way he's wearing that holster," Verkan Vall said. "Has the conveyer gone back, yet?" When the policeman nodded, he continued: "When it returns, take him to the First Level. I hope they bring up the sleep-drug with the next load. When you get him back, take him to Dhergabar by strato-rocket immediately, and make sure he gets back alive. I want him questioned under narco-hypnosis by a regular Paratime Commission psycho-technician, in the presence of Chief Tortha Karf and some responsible Commission official. This is going to be hot stuff."

Within an hour, the whole force was assembled in the temple. The wooden screen had presented no problem—it slid easily to one side—and the big idol floated on antigravity in the middle of the temple. Verkan Vall was looking anxiously at his watch.

"It's about two hours to sunset," he said, to Stranor Sleth. "But as you pointed out, these Hulguns aren't astronomers, and it's a bit cloudy. I wish Crannar Jurth would call in with something definite."

Another twenty minutes passed. Then the man at the radio came out into the temple.

"O. K.!" he called. "The man at Crannar Jurth's called in. Crannar Jurth contacted him with a midget radio he has up his sleeve; he's in the palace courtyard now. They haven't brought out the victims, yet, but Kurchuk has just been carried out on his throne to that platform in front of the citadel. Big crowd gathering in the inner courtyard; more in the streets outside. Palace gates are wide open."

"That's it!" Verkan Vall cried. "Form up; the parade's starting. Brannad, you and Tammand and Stranor and I in front; about ten men with paralyzers a little behind us. Then Yat-Zar, about ten feet off the ground, and then the others. Forward—*ho-o!*"

They emerged from the temple and started down the broad roadway toward the palace. There was not much of a crowd, at first. Most of Zurb had flocked to the palace earlier; the lucky ones in the courtyard and the late comers outside. Those whom they did meet stared at them in open-mouthed amazement, and then some, remembering their doubts and blasphemies, began howling for forgiveness. Others—a substantial majority—realizing that it would be upon King Kurchuk that the real weight of Yat-Zar's six hands would fall, took to their heels, trying to put as much distance as possible between them and the palace before the blow fell.

As the procession approached the palace gates, the crowds were thicker, made up of those who had been unable to squeeze themselves inside. The panic was worse, here, too. A good many were trampled and hurt in the rush to escape, and it became necessary to use paralyzers to clear a way. That made it worse: everybody was sure that Yat-Zar was striking sinners dead left and right.

Fortunately, the gates were high enough to let the god through without losing altitude appreciably. Inside, the mob surged back, clearing a way across the courtyard. It was only necessary to paralyze a few here, and the levitated idol and its priestly attendants advanced toward the stone platform, where the king sat on his throne, flanked by court functionaries and black-robed priests of Muz-Azin. In front of this, a rank of Chuldun archers had been drawn up.

"Horv; move Yat-Zar forward about a hundred feet and up about fifty," Verkan Vall directed. "Quickly!"

As the six-armed anthropomorphic idol rose and moved closer toward its saurian rival, Verkan Vall drew his needler, scanning the assemblage around the throne anxiously.

"*Where is the wicked King?*" a voice thundered—the voice of Stranor Sleth, speaking into a midget radio tuned to the loudspeaker inside the idol. "*Where is the blasphemer and desecrator, Kurchuk?*"

"There's Labdurg, in the red tunic, beside the throne," Tammand Drav whispered. "And that's Ghromdur, the Muz-Azin high priest, beside him."

Verkan Vall nodded, keeping his eyes on the group on the platform. Ghromdur, the high priest of Muz-Azin, was edging backward and reaching under his robe. At the same time, an officer shouted an order, and the Chuldun archers drew arrows from their quivers and fitted them to their bowstrings. Immediately, the ultrasonic paralyzers of the advancing paratimers went into action, and the mercenaries began dropping.

"*Lay down your weapons, fools!*" the amplified voice boomed at them. "*Lay down your weapons or you shall surely die! Who are you, miserable wretches, to draw bows against Me?*"

Illustration

At first a few, then all of them, the Chulduns lowered or dropped their weapons and began edging away to the sides. At the center, in front of the throne, most of them had been knocked out. Verkan Vall was still watching the Muz-Azin high priest intently; as Ghromdur raised his arm, there was a flash and a puff of smoke from the front of Yat-Zar—the paint over the collapsed nickel was burned off, but otherwise the idol was undamaged. Verkan Vall swung up his needler and rayed Ghromdur dead; as the man in the green-faced black robes fell, a blaster clattered on the stone platform.

"Is that your puny best, Muz-Azin?" the booming voice demanded. *"Where is your high priest now?"*

"Horv; face Yat-Zar toward Muz-Azin," Verkan Vall said over his shoulder, drawing his blaster with his left hand. Like all First Level people, he was ambidextrous, although, like all paratimers, he habitually concealed the fact while outtime. As the levitated idol swung slowly to look down upon its enemy on the built-up cart, Verkan Vall aimed the blaster and squeezed.

Illustration

In a spot less than a millimeter in diameter on the crocodile idol's side, a certain number of neutrons in the atomic structure of the stone from which it was carved broke apart, becoming, in effect, atoms of hydrogen. With a flash and a bang, the idol burst and vanished. Yat-Zar gave a dirty laugh and turned his back on the cart, which was now burning fiercely facing King Kurchuk again.

"Get your hands up, all of you!" Verkan Vall shouted, in the First Level language, swinging the stubby muzzle of the blaster and the knob-tipped twin tubes of the needler to cover the group around the throne, "Come forward, before I start blasting!"

Labdurg raised his hands and stepped forward. So did two of the priests of Yat-Zar. They were quickly seized by Paratime Policemen who swarmed up onto the platform and disarmed. All three were carrying sigma-ray needlers, and Labdurg had a blaster as well.

King Kurchuk was clinging to the arms of his throne, a badly frightened monarch trying desperately not to show it. He was a big man, heavy-shouldered, black-bearded; under ordinary circumstances he would probably have cut an imposing figure, in his gold-washed mail and his golden crown. Now his face was a dirty gray, and he was biting nervously at his lower lip. The others on the platform were in even worse state. The Hulgun nobles were grouped together, trying to disassociate themselves from both the king and the priests of Muz-Azin. The latter were staring in a daze at the blazing cart from which their idol had just been blasted. And the dozen men who were to have done the actual work of the torture-sacrifice had all dropped their whips and were fairly gibbering in fear.

Yat-Zar, manipulated by the robed paratimer, had taken a position directly above the throne and was lowering slowly. Kurchuk stared up at the massive idol descending toward him, his knuckles white as he clung to the arms of his throne. He managed to hold out until he could feel the weight of the idol pressing on his head. Then, with a scream, he hurled himself from the throne and rolled forward almost to the edge of the platform. Yat-Zar moved to one side, swung slightly and knocked the throne toppling, and then settled down on the platform. To Kurchuk, who was rising cautiously on his hands and knees, the big idol seemed to be looking at him in contempt.

"*Where are my holy priests, Kurchuk?*" Stranor Sleth demanded in to his sleeve-hidden radio. "*Let them be brought before me, alive and unharmed, or it shall be better for you had you never been born!*"

The six priests of Yat-Zar, it seemed, were already being brought onto the platform by one of Kurchuk's nobles. This noble, whose name was Yorzuk, knew a miracle when he saw one, and believed in being on the side of the god with the heaviest artillery. As soon as he had seen Yat-Zar coming through the gate without visible means of support, he had hastened to the dungeons with half a dozen of his personal retainers and ordered the release of the six captives. He was now escorting them onto the platform, assuring them that he had always been a faithful servant of Yat-Zar and had been deeply grieved at his sovereign's apostasy.

"*Hear my word, Kurchuk,*" Stranor Sleth continued through the loud-speaker in the idol. "*You have sinned most vilely against me, and were I a cruel god, your fate would be such as no man has ever before suffered. But I am a merciful god; behold, you may gain forgiveness in my sight. For thirty days, you shall neither eat meat nor drink wine, nor shall you wear gold nor fine raiment, and each day shall you go to my temple and beseech me for my forgiveness. And on the thirty-first day, you shall set out, barefoot and clad in the garb of a slave, and journey to my temple that is in the mountains over above Yoldav, and there will I forgive you, after you have made sacrifice to me. I, Yat-Zar, have spoken!*"

The king started to rise, babbling thanks.

"*Rise not before me until I have forgiven you!*" Yat-Zar thundered. "*Creep out of my sight upon your belly, wretch!*"

The procession back to the temple was made quietly and sedately along an empty roadway. Yat-Zar seemed to be in a kindly humor; the people of Zurb had no intention of giving him any reason to change his mood. The priests of Muz-Azin and their torturers had been flung into the dungeon. Yorzuk, appointed regent for the duration of Kurchuk's penance, had taken control and was employing Hulgun spearmen and hastily-converted Chuldun archers to restore order and, incidentally, purge a few of his personal enemies and political rivals. The priests, with the three prisoners who had been found carrying First Level weapons among them and Yat-Zar floating triumphantly in front, entered the temple. A few of the devout, who sought admission after them, were told that elaborate and secret rites were being held to cleanse the profaned altar, and sent away.

Verkan Vall and Brannad Klav and Stranor Sleth were in the conveyer chamber, with the Paratime Policemen and the extra priests; along with them were the three prisoners. Verkan Vall pulled off his false beard and turned to face these. He could see that they all recognized him.

"Now," he began, "you people are in a bad jam. You've violated the Paratime Transposition Code, the Commercial Regulation Code, and the First Level Criminal Code, all together. If you know what's good for you, you'll start talking."

"I'm not saying anything till I have legal advice," the man who had been using the local alias of Labdurg replied. "And if you're through searching me, I'd like to have my cigarettes and lighter back."

"Smoke one of mine, for a change," Verkan Vall told him. "I don't know what's in yours beside tobacco." He offered his case and held a light for the prisoner before lighting his own cigarette. "I'm going to be sure you get back to the First Level alive."

The former Overseer of the Kingdom of Zurb shrugged. "I'm still not talking," he said.

"Well, we can get it all out of you by narco-hypnosis, anyhow," Verkan Vall told him. "Besides, we got that man of yours who was here at the temple when we came in. He's being given a full treatment, as a presumed outtime native found in possession of First Level weapons. If you talk now it'll go easier with you."

The prisoner dropped the cigarette on the floor and tramped it out.

"Anything you cops get out of me, you'll have to get the hard way," he said. "I have friends on the First Level who'll take care of me."

"I doubt that. They'll have their hands full taking care of themselves, after this gets out." Verkan Vall turned to the two in the black robes. "Either of you want to say anything?" When they shook their heads, he nodded to a group of his policemen; they were hustled into the conveyer. "Take them to the First Level terminal and hold them till I come in. I'll be along with the next conveyer load."

The conveyer flashed and vanished. Brannad Klav stared for a moment at the circle of concrete floor from whence it had disappeared. Then he turned to Verkan Vall.

"I still can't believe it," he said. "Why, those fellows were First Level paratimers. So was that priest, Ghromdur: the one you rayed."

"Yes, of course. They worked for your rivals, the Fourth Level Mineral Products Syndicate; the outfit that was trying to get your Proto-Aryan Sector fissionables franchise away from you. They operate on this sector already; have the petroleum franchise for the Chuldun country, east of the Caspian Sea. They export to some of these internal-combustion-engine sectors, like Europo-American. You know, most of the wars they've been fighting, lately, on the Europo-American Sector have been, at least in part, motivated by rivalry for oil fields. But now that the Europo-Americans have begun to release nuclear energy, fissionables have become more important than oil. In less than a century, it's predicted that atomic energy will replace all other forms of power. Mineral Products Syndicate wanted to get a good source of supply for uranium, and your Proto-Aryan Sector franchise was worth grabbing.

"I had considered something like this as a possibility when Stranor, here, mentioned that tularemia was normally unknown in Eurasia on this sector. That epidemic must have been started by imported germs. And I knew that Mineral Products has agents at the court of the Chuldun emperor, Chombrog: they have to, to protect their oil wells on his eastern frontiers. I spent most of last night checking up on some stuff by video-transcription from the Paratime Commission's microfilm library at Dhergabar. I found out, for one thing, that while there is a King Kurchuk of Zurb on every time-line for a hundred para-years on either side of this one, this is the only time-line on which he married a Princess Darith of Chuldun, and it's the only time-line on which there is any trace of a Chuldun scribe named Labdurg.

"That's why I went to all the trouble of having that Yat-Zar plated with collapsed nickel. If there were disguised paratimers among the Muz-Azin party at Kurchuk's court, I expected one of them to try to blast our idol when we brought it into the palace. I was watching Ghromdur and Labdurg in particular; as soon as Ghromdur used his blaster, I needled him. After that, it was easy."

"Was that why you insisted on sending that automatic viewer on ahead?"

"Yes. There was a chance that they might have planted a bomb in the House of Yat-Zar, here. I knew they'd either do that or let the place entirely alone. I suppose they were so confident of getting away with this that they didn't want to damage the conveyer or the conveyer chamber. They expected to use them, themselves, after they took over your company's franchise."

"Well, what's going to be done about it by the Commission?" Brannad Klav wanted to know.

"Plenty. The syndicate will probably lose their paratime license; any of its officials who had guilty knowledge of this will be dealt with according to law. You know, this was a pretty nasty business."

"You're telling me!" Stranor Sleth exclaimed. "Did you get a look at those whips they were going to use on our people? Pointed iron barbs a quarter-inch long braided into them, all over the lash-ends!"

"Yes. Any punitive action you're thinking about taking on these priests of Muz-Azin—the natives, I mean—will be ignored on the First Level. And that reminds me: you'd better work out a line of policy, pretty soon."

"Well, as for the priests and the torturers, I think I'll tell Yorzuk to have them sold to the Bhunguns, to the east. They're always in the market for galley slaves," Stranor Sleth said. He turned to Brannad Klav. "And I'll want six gold crowns made up, as soon as possible. Strictly Hulgun design, with Yat-Zar religious symbolism, very rich and ornate, all slightly different. When I give Kurchuk absolution, I'll crown him at the altar in the name of Yat-Zar. Then I'll invite in the other five Hulgun kings, lecture them on their religious duties, make them confess their secret doubts, forgive them, and crown them, too. From then on, they can all style themselves as ruling by the will of Yat-Zar."

"And from then on, you'll have all of them eating out of your hand," Verkan Vall concluded. "You know, this will probably go down in Hulgun history as the Reformation of Ghullam the Holy. I've always wondered whether the theory of the divine right of kings was invented by the kings, to establish their authority over the people, or by the priests, to establish *their* authority over the kings. It works about as well one way as the other."

"What I can't understand is this," Brannad Klav said. "It was entirely because of my respect for the Paratime Code that I kept Stranor Sleth from using Fourth Level weapons and other techniques to control these people with a show of apparent miraculous powers. But this Fourth Level Mineral Products Syndicate was operating in violation of the Paratime Code by invading our franchise area. Why didn't they fake up a supernatural reign of terror to intimidate these natives?"

"Ha, exactly because they *were* operating illegally," Verkan Vall replied. "Suppose they had started using needlers and blasters and antigravity and nuclear-energy around here. The natives would have thought it was the power of Muz-Azin, of course, but what would you have thought? You'd have known, as soon as they tried it, that First Level paratimers were working against you, and you'd have laid the facts before the Commission, and this time-line would have been flooded with Paratime Police. They had to conceal their operations not only from the natives, as you do, but also from us. So they didn't dare make public use of First Level techniques.

"Of course, when we came marching into the palace with that idol on antigravity, they knew, at once, what was happening. I have an idea that they only tried to blast that idol to create a diversion which would permit them to escape—if they could have got out of the palace, they'd have made their way, in disguise, to the nearest Mineral Products Syndicate conveyer and transposed out of here. I realized that they could best delay us by blasting our idol, and that's why I had it plated with collapsed nickel. I think that where they made their mistake was in allowing Kurchuk to have those priests arrested, and insisting on sacrificing them to Muz-Azin. If it hadn't been for that, the Paratime Police wouldn't have been brought into this, at all.

"Well, Stranor, you'll want to get back to your temple, and Brannad and I want to get back to the First Level. I'm supposed to take my wife to a banquet in Dhergabar, tonight, and with the fastest strato-rocket, I'll just barely make it."

CPSIA information can be obtained
at www.ICGtesting.com
Printed in the USA
LVHW112137190722
723892LV00005BA/252